P9-ELX-737

characters created by lauren child

I SLIGHTLY
want to GO home

Grosset & Dunlap
An Imprint of Penguin Group (USA) Inc.

Text based on the script written by Sam Hill.

Illustrations from the TV animations produced by Tiger Aspect.

GROSSET & DUNLAP
Published by the Penguin Group
Penguin Group (USA) Inc., 375 Hudson Street, New York, New York 10014, USA
Penguin Group (Canada), 90 Eglinton Avenue East, Suite 700, Toronto, Ontario M4P 2Y3, Canada
(a division of Pearson Penguin Canada Inc.)
Penguin Books Ltd., 80 Strand, London WC2R 0RL, England
Penguin Group Ireland, 25 St. Stephen's Green, Dublin 2, Ireland
(a division of Penguin Books Ltd.)
Penguin Group (Australia), 250 Camberwell Road, Camberwell, Victoria 3124, Australia
(a division of Pearson Australia Group Pty. Ltd.)
Penguin Books India Pvt. Ltd., 11 Community Centre, Panchsheel Park, New Delhi—110 017, India
Penguin Group (NZ), 67 Apollo Drive, Rosedale, North Shore 0632, New Zealand
(a division of Pearson New Zealand Ltd.)
Penguin Books (South Africa) (Pty.) Ltd., 24 Sturdee Avenue,
Rosebank, Johannesburg 2196, South Africa

Penguin Books Ltd., Registered Offices: 80 Strand, London WC2R 0RL, England

The publisher does not have any control over and does not assume any responsibility for author or third-party websites or their content.

The scanning, uploading, and distribution of this book via the Internet or via any other means without the permission of the publisher is illegal and punishable by law. Please purchase only authorized electronic editions and do not participate in or encourage electronic piracy of copyrighted materials. Your support of the author's rights is appreciated.

Text and illustrations copyright © Lauren Child/Tiger Aspect Productions Limited, 2011.
The Charlie and Lola logo is a trademark of Lauren Child. All rights reserved.
Published by Grosset & Dunlap, a division of Penguin Young Readers Group, 345 Hudson Street,
New York, New York 10014. GROSSET & DUNLAP is a trademark of Penguin Group (USA) Inc. Manufactured in China.

Library of Congress Cataloging-in-Publication Data is available.

ISBN 978-0-448-45461-0   10 9 8 7 6 5 4 3 2 1

I have this little sister, Lola.
She is small and very funny.
Lola is practicing **sleeping** because tonight
she is having her first **sleepover**
at Lotta's house.

When Lola arrives,
Lotta says,
   "YOU'RE HERE, LOLA!
      I have a surprise.
Later we're going to have
   a midnight feast!"

   Lola says,
"Goody! Can we
      have it now?"

But Lotta says,
"No, a midnight feast comes
         at the very end.
We'll do all kinds of fun
      things first."

"We'll play Go Fish . . .

" . . . and dress up . . .

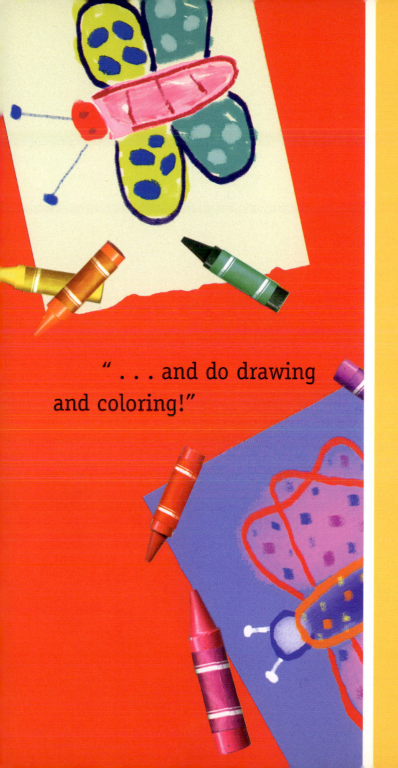

" . . . and do drawing and coloring!"

Afterward Lola says,
"Is it time
for our midnight feast yet?"

But Lotta says,
"No. We've got to
take baths first."

"Lola, why are you brushing your teeth now?" asks Lotta.

Lola says,
"I ALWAYS brush my teeth before the bath.
When do you brush your teeth?"

"Oh," says Lotta. "I always brush my teeth after bath time."

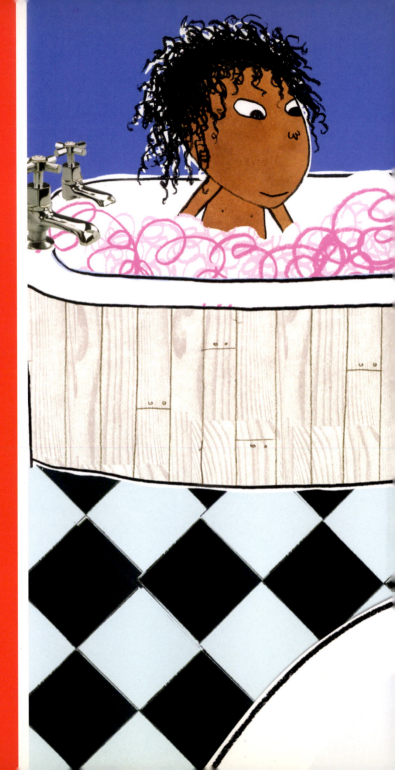

"And after **bath** time,"
Lotta says,
"I watch my pony show."

"Oh," says Lola.
"I usually watch
Pirate Squidbones
because it's
Charlie's **favorite**."

Lotta says,
"Mum says we have
                    ten minutes
before lights out."

So Lola says,
          "Is it time for our
midnight feast yet?"

And Lotta says,
          "Yes! Yes! Yes!"

Finally it's time
        for lights out.

Lotta says,
        "Now let's get
Foxy ready for bed."

"Yes, yes," says Lola.

And Lotta says,
        "Now then, Foxy,
you can sleep over here
        in a special bed.

Time to put out the light.
        Night-night, Lola!"

Lotta switches
off the light, but Lola
turns it **on** again.

Lotta says,
"What's the matter, Lola?"

And Lola says,
"I WANT TO GO HOME!!!"

"Why do you want
to go home?" Lotta asks.

And Lola says,
"I think maybe
it's the floor-bed."

So Lola and Lotta
trade beds.

Lola says, "And I really
need to have Foxy
in bed with me."

So Lotta gets Foxy.
"Here," Lotta says.
"Does that make you
feel more better?"

But Lola says,
     "Everything is
a bit too different.
     We didn't even play
I Went to the Moon.
          Me and Charlie
always play that."

"Okay," says Lotta.
"But how do we play?"

     So Lola says,
     "First we pretend we
are going to the moon.
     Then we take turns
          saying funny
things to bring."

Lotta says,
"I went to the m00n
        and took sunglasses.
Your turn!"

    Lola says,
    "I went to the m00n
and took sunglasses
        and a pony."

Then Lotta says,
    "I went to the
m00n and took sunglasses,
    a pony, and a bird."

Then Lotta says,
"Your turn! Lola? Looola?"
But Lola is fast asleep.
"Oh," says Lotta. "Night-night, Lola."